—
[chapter]

1

Click. Click. Click. It was getting late. Nishell knew it. School was over. Shadows followed her down the sidewalk. If she stopped for much longer she'd miss the bus home. She just wanted to take one more picture, of a flower growing between shards of glass and graffiti on the crumbling pavement.

Click.

"Perfect! That's it!" Nishell said to herself. It was everything she wanted to capture. It showed poverty and cruelty, yet with something beautiful growing out of it. Her mom, Sierra, would love it.

—

Nishell brushed her big brown curls out of her face. Then she carefully put her camera away. The camera was the best thing she owned. She didn't usually bring it to school, but the yearbook club needed an extra camera today. Nishell knew she took the best pictures with her own camera. Many times, her camera was like her best friend. It helped her express what she thought and felt.

For a mandatory punishment from Mr. Crandall, the guidance counselor, YC wasn't so bad. He assigned the after-school club activity when Nishell skipped gym for the tenth time. Nishell made the best of it. Her long-time secret crush, Jackson, was in YC. And she was making some tight friends. Nishell never would have gotten to know brainiacs like Kiki and Tia. She was even getting along with the more popular girls like Marnyke, one of the hottest girls in school, and Sherise, Kiki's twin sister.

That said, no one was allowed to touch her camera except Nishell. She'd worked a whole year serving ice cream after school to buy it. She wasn't about to let anyone take it or break it. Her mom wanted her to save her money. But after a year of arguing about it, Nishell paid for that camera in cash.

Ms. Okoro, the YC advisor, made a surprise announcement at the meeting today. Nishell had won a district art award for her "Beauty in the Hood" photo series. Tia, Kiki, and Sherise clapped and screamed for Nishell. Even Marnyke seemed sort of happy for her.

"Nice photos," Marnyke said. "I kinda like them."

"You can all see Nishell's pictures next week. The school is hanging them in the first floor hallway for the rest of the year," Ms. O said. "Congratulations,

Nishell! Let's find a place in the year-book for a photo of Nishell next to one of her photos."

Nishell's own pictures! "Oh, thank you, Ms. O!" Nishell said. It was a good day, for once.

Nishell started walking to catch the bus. She was so hyped. She couldn't wait to tell her mom about her award and photos hanging in the school. Sierra would be damn proud. Even better, it was Thursday, her mom's night off. Nishell, her mom, and her brother, Ka'lon, would have dinner together. They might even watch a movie. Best of all, once her mom heard, maybe she would finally want to talk to Nishell about her photography. Maybe she would stop thinking it was a waste of time and money.

Nishell walked faster. She couldn't miss this bus. The next one didn't come for another thirty minutes. It would be dark by then. She turned the corner. The bus was pulling away! She sprinted after it, her backpack bouncing off her back and her arms waving wildly. It wasn't going to stop for her! She was about to give up when the bus finally stopped.

Nishell quickly hopped on. She gave the driver her biggest, flirty out-of-breath smile. Someone once told Nishell her smile was brighter than the stars. Probably because her teeth sparkled against her smooth, dark skin. The bus driver frowned back at her. "Guess he doesn't think my smile is so dazzling," Nishell thought. She saw an open seat and went for it.

"Hey! Home girl! I done made the driver stop for you. Don't I get some love?" a voice beside her said.

Nishell opened her mouth to say she didn't owe nobody nothing. Then she saw the bluest eyes she'd ever seen.

Nishell knew those eyes. She'd been obsessing over them since seventh grade, although he didn't know it. It was Jackson Beauford. Too bad he always belonged to another girl, or two, or three. It was probably best to just be friends with Jackson. Oh well.

"I ... I ... uh. Thanks, Jackson," Nishell stammered. She blushed. She didn't usually act like this around boys. Not even Jackson. Flirting was more her style. She wasn't supposed to flirt with Jackson anymore, though. He'd been going with Marnyke for a week now.

Jackson gave her his trademark smile. The one where his mouth curved up, only on one side. It made Nishell melt. She always forgot it made every other girl in school melt too. Especially Marnyke. Jackson had always been a flirt.

"No prob, girl. You know I got your back," he told her.

Nishell smirked. She couldn't resist. "Yeah. But just because mine is so fine."

Jackson looked her over. "You got that right, girl. I don't know nobody with such a nice big behind," he teased.

He couldn't get away with that. Nishell couldn't let him know she was crushing.

"And I don't know nobody with such a big head ... or a big mouth," Nishell said.

Jackson looked upset. "Nah, home girl. You know it was a compliment. You a dime. For real."

Nishell didn't respond for a second. She knew she was a little bigger than most girls. That never stopped her from flirting. In fact most guys seemed to like her better than prissy thin girls like Marnyke. She might not be like the other girls Jackson chased, but at least he was interested.

Jackson still looked unhappy. Nishell grinned and shook her curls. She should tell him the truth. "I know I'm a dime. I was just makin' sure you know it too."

Jackson smiled. "You had me goin' there."

"Who do you think I am? Some chick that needs primpin' day and night? I got better things to do than just you," Nishell said.

"Nah. You better than that," he told her. He seemed to be thinking for a second. "Hey, you be 'round later tonight, right? Make some time for me. I'm thinkin' I should be hangin' more with a girl like you."

A week ago Nishell would have said yes, no question. But then, a week ago Marnyke and Jackson weren't almost an official couple. Nishell really liked Jackson, but she didn't want drama, especially not girlfriend drama. If Nishell went out with Jackson, she knew nobody in YC would even look at her anymore.

She'd be called a no-good, double-crossing, back-stabbing slut. She didn't need that right now.

"I don't know, Jackson. Don't you got somebody else you hangin' with?" Nishell asked. She felt bad about flirting with Jackson now. She just couldn't help it sometimes.

"Nah. I'm free as a bird. Don't listen to what you hear," Jackson told her. Nishell felt the bus jerk to a stop.

"I don't know, Jackson. I don't think it's a good idea," Nishell told him.

Jackson jumped up. "Don't you worry, girl. I'll be seein' you later tonight!"

Before Nishell could say anything else Jackson hopped off the bus.

For the rest of the ride Nishell wondered what she was going to do. This was what she'd wanted, always. Nishell and Jackson had always flirted, but he'd never made a move. Until now. What if

Marnyke found out? Nishell didn't want trouble. She almost missed her stop she was thinking so hard.

When Nishell got to her house she could smell dinner even before she opened the back door. What was going on? Her mom didn't usually start cooking for another hour or two. Sierra liked to relax on her night off from her job as a telephone counselor at the Tenth Street Shelter.

But all of Nishell's questions drifted away with a sniff. Meatballs and home-made spaghetti. She remembered her award and smiled. Tonight was going to be a good night. She pushed open the door. Instead of her mom stirring the pasta, she was racing from the kitchen to the dining room.

"Where have you been, Nishell?" Sierra snapped. "You're late."

Nishell couldn't believe it. "What's all this?" she asked as all of her troubles came rushing back.

"I expected you to be home an hour ago, young lady," Sierra told her. "We're having some friends over for dinner tonight. You were supposed to help me get ready."

"You serious, Mom?" Nishell asked, though she already knew. In their house, "having friends over" meant her mom had invited some homeless people from the shelter. She did it once a month or so.

"Mooommm. This is our one night a week to eat as a family! Don't you even care? You didn't even ask what's goin' on with me." Nishell crossed her arms.

Her mom didn't turn around. "Stop giving me sass, young lady. You know we gotta do our part to help. Give back what we got."

"Seems like you been givin' everything away forever," Nishell said under her breath.

Her mother spun around. Pink spots stood out against her white cheeks. Guess she'd heard what Nishell had said.

"Miss Nishell Saunders," Sierra told her. "I mean it when I say get your butt ready, because we *will* be having guests over. Whether you like it or not. I want you on your best behavior. No rattling anyone's ears off. Not everyone wants to hear 'bout you," her mom said. She turned back to the stove.

Nishell couldn't believe it. It was the one night she'd been looking forward to all week. Her mom had to go and ruin it by inviting people over! Even worse, homeless people. Nobody else Nishell knew had homeless people over for dinner. At school homeless people were a joke. If anyone at school knew, they'd just laugh at her for being such a loser. Sierra probably didn't even care that Nishell had won an award today. Lately it didn't seem like her mom cared about Nishell at all.

"For once, why can't you think 'bout me!" Nishell shouted. She ran to her room before her mom could say anything. Nishell made sure to slam the door extra hard behind her.

When the door stopped rattling, Nishell headed for her bed. She lay down and stared at the ceiling. How could her mom not even care about her? It seemed like all her mom cared about was helping other people.

Nishell hated when homeless people came over for dinner. They were always so nice and polite. The worst part was when her mom always reminded her that their family used to be homeless too. Nishell was always, always trying to forget. She'd been trying to forget it since she was seven.

Before then her family hadn't lived anywhere for long. She had never been to school before. When she finally started school, they put her in first grade. She was a year older than the other first-graders. But most of them knew more than she did.

At school, she was asked to draw her home. Everyone else drew apartments or houses with fences. Nishell didn't know what to draw. She sat at her desk looking at the paper. One girl even asked, "What's wrong with you? Don't you got a home? Maybe that's why you're such a weirdo." Nishell was so embarrassed. She remembered hiding in the bathroom during lunch.

Everything was better now. Nishell, her mom, and Ka'lon had their own house. They hadn't moved since she was in first grade. And no one knew anything about her life before then. Nishell

—

wanted to keep it that way. That's why she never told anyone her birthday. Then they would know she started school late. Nishell was eighteen, almost nineteen. Way too old for a junior in high school. Whenever anybody asked, she lied.

Nishell sighed. She was being selfish, she knew. She knew lots of people had helped her mom get through the hard times with her and Ka'lon. But if everybody *now* knew, people would make fun of her. She might lose all her friends.

From her bed Nishell heard the front door open. She sat up. Voices came down the hallway. Looked like their guests were here. Nishell got up. If her mom had to drag her out of her room it would just mean a worse fight later. Plus she was hungry. She didn't want to miss dinner.

Nishell took a deep breath before she opened her door. She could do this. Lots of people had come over and no one had found out about her secret yet, right?

Nishell opened the door. It took all of two seconds for her mouth to drop to the floor. Standing outside her door was one of the hottest seniors in her school. And one of her first friends ever, Cyril Davis.

If he was here for dinner did that mean his family was living at the shelter? Nishell's mom didn't have other people over for dinner. Said she'd have other people over when the shelter was empty.

Either Nishell's mom had changed her mind or Cyril was homeless.

"What are you doin' here?" Nishell blurted out.

"Hey, Shell," Cyril said with a smile. "Nice of you to have folks like us over for dinner."

Nishell didn't know what to say. She leaned on the doorframe.

"Serious. You lost?" Nishell asked. "I must be trippin'. You can't be here for dinner."

She'd known Cyril forever practically. He lived a few blocks away. Or used to. Nishell had even baby-sat his sister, Alisha. She was the same age as Ka'lon.

Alisha peaked out from behind Cyril. "We ain't lost. Don't you want us to be here for dinner, Shell?"

Before Nishell said anything, her mom called everyone into the kitchen. "Dinner's up! Come get it while it's hot."

Alisha rushed to Nishell's side. "Come on, Shell! I wanna sit by you."

Nishell walked into the kitchen in a daze. How had this happened? She knew Mr. Davis had been out of work, but it still didn't make sense. It was too bad. Now Nishell knew why her mother wanted to help. Still, Cyril was one of the hottest guys in school. He had been one of her best friends when she was little. Definitely one of the cutest guys to sit at Nishell's dinner table. She wasn't going to complain, at least for tonight.

"I'll help," Nishell told her mom. Nishell started dishing up the spaghetti.

Her mom gave her a funny look. Nishell shook her head. Nishell wasn't mad at her mom anymore. She had to know what happened to the Davises.

"All right, baby. I'll let it go if you will," Nishell's mom said. She handed Nishell a plate.

They were all sitting when Ka'lon finally came into the room. He was always late for dinner. "Probably playing video games," Nishell thought.

Ka'lon sat at the table "Yo. What's Lish's family doing here, Mom?" he asked.

"Ka'lon. Shut up!" Nishell winced. He knew better than to ask. Even though she'd done the same thing to Cyril a minute earlier.

Mr. Davis sighed. He put his fork down. "It's okay, Nishell. We're all friends here."

Mrs. Davis squeezed his hand. "We're just a bit down on our luck."

Cyril snorted. "Yeah, you can say that."

Mrs. Davis turned to Nishell's mom. "It's just that with our bills, we couldn't keep the house anymore. We're just staying at the shelter till we get back on our feet."

Nishell's mom smiled. "I know. That's why I invited you. We used to be in the same spot, not too many years ago."

Nishell looked at her plate. Her secret was out. She'd even hid it from Cyril. Her oldest friend. Would Cyril tell anyone? What if her mother found out she'd been hiding everything?

"Whatever," Ka'lon said. Twelve-year-olds usually didn't care about stories.

Ka'lon was more clueless than most stupid little brothers too. "I jus' wanna know if Cyril will play ball with me after dinner. Just me and you. Will ya? Please?"

"Yeah," Cyril said between bites of spaghetti. "Be happy to."

"That's not fair!" Alisha said.

"Hey, Lish," Nishell said. "I can paint your nails if you want."

"Ooo!" Alisha squealed. "Can we play dress up and take pictures too?"

"Sure, that'd be fun," Nishell said.

"Hey, Shell," Cyril said.

Nishell froze. Would he tell her mother the truth?

"Looks like Alisha's getting a good deal with the pictures. Heard you won an award today at school. For your photos. Hear they are gonna hang in the school hall. Pretty cool."

Nishell blushed. Cyril just called her cool!

Her mom gasped. "Really, baby? That's great!"

Mrs. Davis smiled. "You should tell us all about them. If Cyril thinks they're cool, they must be something."

Nishell smiled. This dinner definitely was turning out better than she'd ever hoped.

She told them about the award and what Ms. Okoro has said about putting one of her pictures in the yearbook. And for the rest of the meal everyone talked about her pictures. They all wanted to hear more about them. Alisha said that when she became a famous model Nishell would be her only photographer. By the end of the meal everybody was laughing and enjoying the evening.

After dinner Nishell was more than happy to clean up the dishes. Cyril rolled up his shirt sleeves and offered to help her instantly. He said it was time for everyone else to relax. What a good guy he was.

Once everyone left the room, Cyril turned to Nishell.

"Shell, you can't tell nobody 'bout this. Understand? I got a rep to keep."

Nishell nodded. "Obvi. What, you think I want anybody knowing 'bout this? Or 'bout us?"

Cyril shrugged. "Guess not. I never knew you was a street girl till now. And I known you forever."

Nishell was quiet. She didn't need any grief from anybody right now. This would give everybody something to talk about. She wondered if there were other kids at school hiding secrets too. She'd never thought of it that way before.

"Are there a lot of people like you now? At school, I mean?" Nishell asked. He would know.

Cyril shrugged. "Some. I seen them 'round the shelter a few times."

———

Nishell looked sideways at Cyril. This was probably the last thing he wanted to talk about. Lord knows it had been years since she'd slept on a cot. She still never wanted to talk about it.

She asked Cyril what he planned to be doing in the fall. Graduation was in a few months. He was a senior after all.

Cyril started talking real fast. He played football last fall. Maybe headed for a scholarship too. If he kept his grades up. Nishell noticed his muscles stretched out his shirt a little bit. When he set the last plate down, Nishell saw a dark bruise on his arm. Could that be from football still? That was a while ago.

Before Nishell could ask, the doorbell rang. Her mom was out back, so Nishell ran to get it.

Nishell opened the door. On the other side of the door was Jackson. She had forgotten all about the bus ride earlier.

She'd been waiting for Jackson to visit her forever! Nishell really didn't think he would show. Why? Why did he pick tonight?

"So, you gonna let me in?" Jackson asked with his half smile.

"I told you before. I got a lot of homework. Come back tomorrow instead?" Nishell whispered.

Jackson leaned toward Nishell. "Aw, come on, girl, just for one minute? I came all the way over."

Jackson was already halfway in the house. Nishell didn't know what to do. Cyril's voice came from down the hall. He was looking for her brother.

Jackson turned his head. "Who's that?"

"Nothin'. Nobody," she said quickly. "Must be the TV or somethin'."

Jackson looked past her. "You sure? You're not jackin' me, are ya?"

—

"Yes. And no." She pushed Jackson back out the door. Nishell could hear Cyril coming her way. She started talking really loud and fast. "Okay. Lots of homework. Gotta go. See you tomorrow at school. Bye!"

She slammed the door shut before Jackson could say another word.

Cyril walked up. "Who was that? And do you know where your bro is? I gotta get my b-ball on."

"It was nobody," Nishell lied. "And I think Ka'lon's probably in the back ready to go."

Cyril shrugged. He walked away. Nishell giggled and leaned on the wall. She had won an award for her photographs. Her mom couldn't wait to see her pictures. Hot guys were at her door and in her house. What a day! But then her heart sank. Her biggest secret was out.

[chapter]

3

At school the next morning, Nishell was dragging. After the Davises left, Nishell remembered she had a big chemistry quiz the next day. She stayed up half the night studying. She needed to pass. She was practically failing all of her classes. She was pretty sure she had no chance of getting into art school unless she passed something.

Nishell slumped in her chair during history class. It was the most boring thing. She wondered if anyone would say anything if she put her head down on her desk. It wasn't like Mr. Sanchez was paying attention anyway.

"Psst. *Chica!*" Tia whispered. She always had Nishell's back. Tia knew without looking when Nishell was daydreaming instead of taking notes. Girl had eyes in the back of her head.

"What? I got it. Something about the Mexican War. The Alamo and all that crap," Nishell snapped.

"*Dios!* Do I care? I know this. *Chica,* have you heard what everyone's been saying?" Tia asked.

Tia wanted to gossip? This must be big. Nishell sat forward.

"No! What? Spill."

"Don't you know? I heard you had Cyril Davis over at your house last night," Tia whispered.

"What?" Nishell said loudly. Her heart started racing.

Did that mean everyone knew her secret too? What would she do?

She got a glare from Mr. Sanchez. Nishell pretended to take notes until he turned back around.

"I also heard you guys were messing around too," Tia said.

Nishell laughed out loud. Her and Cyril? Sure he was hot, but she'd known him forever. It wasn't like that. She was relieved. If stupid rumors were spreading about her and Cyril, for sure nobody knew about Nishell's past.

She got another stare from the teacher. "Nishell, one more time and it's to the office," Mr. Sanchez said sternly.

Tia kept talking, though.

"For real. Stay away from him, *chica*. That guy is bad news. I heard last week Cyril was cutting class 'cause he deals. And my cousin, Mario, he says he's seen

31

Cyril in fights. He's always got cuts and bruises and stuff."

"He just came over to watch Ka'lon," Nishell told Tia. "I had a ton of homework to do."

Tia shrugged. "Sure, I believe you. Just watch yourself." Tia didn't sound like she believed Nishell.

The bell rang.

"Not to worry 'bout me. Not with Cyril anyway," Nishell said as they walked out of class.

Nishell hoped Tia's words would be the end of it. A senior with a junior was big news though. Hell, Nishell usually loved to hear the scoop. But not when it was about her. Before lunch Nishell was asked fifty times if she was hanging with Cyril.

Then another question popped up. Was she two-timin' Jackson too? Nishell couldn't believe how much buzz she had stirred, but it seemed her secret was still safe. And it felt pretty good to be the center of attention. Even if it wasn't for something good.

When the lunch bell rang, Nishell walked quickly out of class. At her locker she decided she wasn't going to sit at her usual table with the YC gang. Maybe she'd sit at a table in the farthest corner of the lunchroom instead.

"Hey, girl! What's kickin' with the hottest junior I know?"

The voice came from the other side of Nishell's locker. It was Marnyke. Nishell shut her locker. Sherise was standing there too.

"You talkin' to me?" Nishell asked. Marnyke surely heard about last night from all the chat. What was she gonna say? Was she jealous? What's with Sherise?

"Oh, yeah, I be talkin' to you, girl! You got the whole school buzzin'. It ain't even noon yet! I hear even Kiki knows,"

Marnyke said. She moved closer to Nishell.

"That be some serious business," Sherise said.

Nishell played it cool. "Know about what?"

"Don't take me for no fool, girl," Marnyke said.

"You had Cyril *and* Jackson over at your house last night? Two hot guys. One night. Girl you are playin' somebody," Marnyke said.

"You playin' with fire," Sherise said.

"I wasn't playin' nobody," Nishell said. "Cyril was babysittin' my bro. I had homework. Jackson only stopped by to grab some chemistry notes. For the quiz today."

Marnyke rolled her eyes. "Yeah. We know you and Jackson got chemistry. It's only 'cause he ain't man enough to handle real women."

Sherise laughed. "Mar. Chill. Ain't her fault she's got them after her."

Marnyke shrugged. "What? Oh, who gives a freakin' rip. I was just playin' my friend Nishell. I ain't interested in high school boys no more. She can have him."

Nishell had to escape. What if this went on all during lunch? She couldn't listen anymore. Nishell just couldn't go into that lunchroom. No one even cared about her photography award!

"I gotta study for that chemistry quiz, sisters," Nishell told them. "See you at YC."

Nishell walked as quickly as she could away from her locker. Had she pulled it off with Marnyke and Sherise? She couldn't look back. She might blow it. Maybe she'd eat outside instead. It was cold, but not that cold.

"Hey, Nishell!" Kiki waved.

Nishell sighed. Now what will Kiki say? She ignored her and walked faster.

"Hey, I saw your photos!" Kiki yelled after her. "Absolutely awesome. You gotta see it, girl."

Nishell stopped and turned. She wanted to say thanks, but Kiki was gone. "Oh well," Nishell thought. "At least somebody remembered about the photos." Nishell leaned against the wall. Here was as good as anywhere, she figured. She sat down and unwrapped her sandwich.

"Yo," Cyril called from down the hallway. He walked up and sat next to Nishell. "You heard?"

Nishell laughed. "From everybody and their momma. Guess you been gettin' it too?"

Cyril shrugged. "A bit. No biggie. At least none of it's true. Thanks for keepin' quiet, girl."

Nishell looked at him. "Of course. You keepin' quiet for me too. We gotta stick this out together."

She noticed his jaw was bruised and swollen. "Speaking of stickin' together. Where'd you get that?" She pointed at the bruise. "My brother been beatin' on you?" Nishell joked.

Cyril turned away. "Girl, it ain't nothin'. Just forget it. I would step up off it. Not your business."

Nishell didn't know what to say. His stomach rumbled. Nishell could see he was skipping lunch. She didn't say a word and handed him part of her sandwich.

Cyril took a bite. "Thanks. You heard the shelter might stop servin' dinner every night?"

Nishell gasped. "What? Why?" The shelter had always served dinner. Her family ate there all the time when she was little.

Cyril shrugged. "No money. Don't know what we're gonna do. It's the one place we can get a full meal each day. We ain't the only ones, neither. Lotta people gonna go hungry."

No way. Nishell never knew the shelter was hurting that bad. Sure her mom didn't get paid much. She even worked a second job. But stopping dinner? That was just plain wrong. Nishell knew she had to do something to help.

Before she could ask Cyril more about it, he hopped up. "Well, gotta go. See you 'round, Shell. We cool, right?"

Nishell was in a daze the rest of the day. She had so many things on her mind. Cyril. Jackson. The girls. The chemistry quiz that she prayed she passed. And the shelter. She just couldn't let it go. It had been her home at one time. Sure she didn't want anyone to know. But she couldn't just do nothing. It was sad that some people only ate once a day. Nishell knew her mom having people over for dinner made a difference.

Nishell was still thinking about the shelter's problems as she walked to YC after school.

"Yo, home girl! Daydreaming 'bout me or somethin'?" Jackson came up right in front of her.

Nishell half smiled. "Not today. I've had enough of you for a while."

"Oh yeah? I been hearin' 'bout Cyril. What's up with you and him?" Jackson started walking backwards in front of her. Nishell was annoyed. She wanted to get to YC.

"What's it to you, Jackson? We just friends. No benefits. He was babysitting my brother. End of story," she said.

"For real? You're not into him? 'Cause Marnyke said …"

Nishell stopped walking. "For real, Jackson. Why do you care? You want to hang with me or what? 'Cause I ain't gonna be jerked around. If you're done with Marnyke and wanna do somethin', say so."

Jackson looked stunned. But Nishell wasn't done. She was tired of all of the stupid talk. Well, what she really wanted was to give everybody something real to talk about. She'd have to get Jackson to man up for that though.

"I got better things to think about," Nishell told him. "So speak up or back up offa me."

Jackson's mouth hung open long enough for Nishell to smirk. She side-stepped him and kept walking. After three steps Jackson ran up next to her.

"You know what? Yeah," Jackson said.

Nishell wasn't letting him off easy. She'd seen other girls get played by Jackson. "Yeah what?"

"Yeah. I'm done with Marnyke. I wanna go out with you, Miss Nishell. Tonight," Jackson said.

Nishell smiled. "You're on, boy."

The two of them walked into the YC meeting. They were late and everyone stared at them. Jackson walked to the back with the other boys. He sat next to Darnell. Nishell saw all the boys fist bump.

Nishell sat up front with the girls. She whispered to Tia, "I got big plans tonight. With Jackson."

Tia's face looked surprised. Nishell knew all the other girls heard. Nishell was watching Marnyke. Was she going to flip? Marnyke shrugged and shook her head. Guess she and Jackson were really over.

Sherise leaned forward. "Marnyke got a call from a college boy after lunch!

Jackson ain't nothing no more. Can you believe it?"

Ms. Okoro interrupted Sherise. "Could we all listen up please? Every after-school organization has been asked to think of ways to raise money to help the community. Each group will present its fund-raising idea at the assembly next week. The school will pick the idea they think will help the most people in the community. So, does anyone have any ideas?"

"Pay my way to college! I'm from the community," Darnell yelled from the back.

Everyone laughed.

"Probably something that helps more people than just you, Darnell," Ms. O said.

"We could, like, paint a mural or something," a girl named Misha offered.

"How would that raise money, Misha?" Marnyke asked.

"What about something for the Tenth Street Shelter?" Nishell offered. "They need money and it's just down the block. I was thinking of going there this weekend. I can check it out."

"Great idea, Nishell," Ms. Okoro said.

"I'll go too!" Sherise said. "We should make it a YC field trip. You come too, Marnyke."

Marnyke rolled her eyes. "That's our YC president."

"I'll go," Tia said.

Then everybody wanted to go. Nishell was thrilled. The heat was off her for the day. Even if she had a date with Jackson later. For now, she was making a difference already. She couldn't wait to tell her mom about her idea.

Nishell asked everyone to meet at 11:00 Saturday morning a block from the shelter. She would make sure there would be something they could do to help.

—

As everyone was leaving YC, Ms. O pulled Nishell aside.

"I've been thinking," Ms. Okoro said. "You've got real talent, Nishell. Why don't you try making your volunteer experience into an article for the newspaper? If it's really good, I might be able to squeeze it into the yearbook too."

Nishell's eyes got big. "For real, Ms. O?"

"I'll do my best, Nishell. Why don't you give it a shot? Maybe it can be a part of your portfolio for art school some day," Ms. O said.

Nishell smiled. Helping people and doing art? What could go wrong?

4

Nishell unlocked the front door. "Ka'lon! I'm home!" she yelled. He usually got home from school a few minutes before Nishell did.

She walked to the kitchen to get a drink. Ka'lon didn't respond. He didn't even holler at her. That was pretty weird. Usually he at least popped his head out of his door to say hi.

"Ka'lon? You here?" Nishell called.

Again, she got no response. She peeked in Ka'lon's room. He was nowhere in sight. She looked out back at the basketball court. He wasn't there either. Maybe he went down the street to play with Tomas. He did that sometimes, even though he was supposed to wait until Nishell got home before going anywhere.

She was about to go down the street when her phone buzzed. It was a text from Cyril. "Hey Girl. Heard bout your hot date. I have Ka'lon 4 some man time 2nite. Have fun."

Nishell shook her head. Cyril had watched Ka'lon before. He'd never picked Ka'lon up without asking first, though. Nishell's mom probably wouldn't even be mad. She said Ka'lon needed male role models. Whatever that meant.

Nishell took a deep breath. She couldn't complain too much. Now she had tons of time to get ready for her big night. She was going to need help. She called Tia.

The phone rang. And rang again. Damn, Tia must be working. As usual. It was even a Friday night! Her family made her work at that bakery all the time. Tia's voice mail came on. Nishell hung up. She pressed her speed dial again. Tia always picked up on the second call.

"*Qué pasa?* You know I'm at work, *chica*," Tia said, annoyed.

"Tia!" Nishell said. "Hey, girl. You'd best come over. I need help for tonight."

"*Dios.* Okay. I can get my cousin Mario to cover for me. I'll be over in thirty," Tia said.

Nishell hung up the phone. She'd almost forgotten! She had to call the shelter about YC coming to help serve meals tomorrow. She hit another speed dial on her phone. Would her mom pick up?

"Tenth Street Shelter. How can I help you?" It wasn't Nishell's mom. It was

Francis. Nishell smiled. Francis was one of her favorite people at the shelter. He ran the cafeteria. He always had extra treats for Nishell. Francis was the one who said her smile would get her anything she wanted. He always cheered her up when she was down.

"Hey, Francis!" Nishell said.

"Why if it isn't little Shell! How are ya? Still got that smile? Haven't seen you 'round in a minute. Want to talk to your mom?"

"No. Actually, Francis I wanted to talk to you!" Nishell said. "I want to help out tomorrow. For lunch. And I'm bringing my yearbook club friends. That okay?"

"Why, for you girl? Anythin'. I can find somethin' to do with a bunch a youngstas," Francis laughed.

"Perfect, Francis! You won't be sorry! We're also tryin' to think of a way to raise some money for the shelter," Nishell said.

"I never!" Francis sounded surprised. "You heard 'bout our troubles then? Y'all want to help? Kids like you make the community better, Shell."

Nishell gulped. She just hoped she could live up to what Francis thought of her. "Thanks, Francis. See ya tomorrow."

She hung up and shook her head. Too many thoughts swirling around in her head. What would happen if the shelter closed? But what Nishell really needed right now was to let it all go.

Getting ready for her big night would be the perfect distraction. Nishell looked in her closet. It was practically bursting with clothes. After she'd bought her camera, all her work money went to clothes. Colorful clothes. How else was she going get guys to notice?

Nishell picked up a neon yellow shirt. Too much. She threw it over her shoulder. The blue tank top? Too boring. She threw it on the floor. Could she wear a hot pink shirt and purple sneakers? Or heels? She didn't want to be too dressy. Jackson was probably just taking her out for pizza.

By the time Tia showed up, Nishell's bed and floor were piled high with a mess of clothes.

Tia walked in and laughed. "Looks like a tornado went through here! You must be really nervous."

Nishell ran her hands through her curls. "I know! I just don't know what to wear. Nothing looks right."

Tia sifted through the piles. She picked up an orange dress. "I almost need sunglasses this is so bright." She dropped the dress on the bed.

"So what should I wear?" Nishell asked.

Tia picked out a sequined green shirt and Nishell's favorite jeans. "Wear these with your boots."

"Oh!" Nishell squealed. "That's just right!"

"And your hair is already perfect. You are so lucky," Tia sighed.

Nishell nodded. "I got my momma's hair. Curly. I don't even need to relax it like most girls at school."

"Speakin' of girls at school," Nishell continued. "Did you hear? Marnyke says she's done with high school boys. She's got a date with a college man!"

Tia rolled her eyes. "She would. All that girl's got on her mind is boys and lipstick."

Nishell clicked her tongue against her teeth. "Harsh. What you think is on my mind?"

Tia laughed. "I'm not hating on you. Yeah, you're a guy magnet. But you've got something else going on too. You got talent, *chica*. You're gonna be a famous photographer."

"Mmm-hmm," Nishell said. She wasn't paying much attention. She was daydreaming about Jackson while doing her makeup.

"Where's Ka'lon?" Tia asked. "I know my little brother would be all over the place if I had a date."

Nishell played it cool. "Cyril's watchin' him."

Tia looked at Nishell like she was crazy. "You let Cyril Davis watch your twelve-year-old brother? After what I told you? What you know about him that I don't?"

Nishell shrugged. She wanted to tell Tia about him being homeless, but she'd promised not to. Nishell would have to keep her mouth shut for now.

Tia narrowed her eyes. "There's something you're not tellin' me, *chica*. Spill."

"Look," Nishell sighed. "It's a long story. No time right now."

"Oh, right," Tia said sarcastically. "You got more important things. Well whenever you can spare the time for your best *amiga*, over a boy, you let me know." Tia walked out.

"It's not like that," Nishell said. But Tia had already gone out the back door. Nishell picked up her keys to follow her.

The front doorbell rang. It was Jackson. Tia would have to wait. "She doesn't stay mad long anyway," Nishell thought. Nishell opened the door. Her heart sank. She'd put in a lot of work to look fine. Jackson hadn't even changed out of his school clothes. Still wearing an old black T-shirt and loose jeans.

Then Jackson smiled and Nishell decided his clothes didn't matter. She was going out with Jackson Beauford! The boy everybody wanted.

"Hey, baby girl. You ready?" he asked.

"No doubt," Nishell said. She grabbed

her keys and locked the door without looking back.

"We headed to Mio's. Cool with you?" Jackson asked.

Mio's was the local pizza hangout. Everybody went there on Friday nights before going to the teen club. She and Jackson must have talked to ten people before they got a booth! When they did sit down they got the best seat. It was the booth where they could see everyone walking by, and everybody could see them. Jackson even scooted over to Nishell's side.

Darnell walked by and flashed Jackson a thumbs up. Nishell was hyped. Darnell thought, she, Nishell was a catch!

"Hey, baby. You cold?" Jackson asked. He didn't wait for Nishell to say anything. Instead he put an arm around her.

Nishell smiled. Could this night go any better?

—

She was convinced it couldn't. She and Jackson didn't talk a whole lot. Too many people kept coming by to chat. Jackson kept telling everyone he was with a "catch." And that he was lucky to get Nishell "before those other boys." Nishell wasn't sure what he was talking about, but it sounded nice. She was beaming.

Their pizza finally arrived. Hot and steaming. Nishell took her first bite. Delicious! But she didn't want to eat too much. Jackson might think she was a pig.

"Cyril, I want a slice with pepperoni." Nishell heard Ka'lon's voice from behind her. She looked around. There was Cyril with Ka'lon! She leaned around Jackson to get a better look.

"What you doin', Nishell?" Jackson asked.

"My bro is here," Nishell told him without turning around.

"Well forget him. He'll be 'round later," Jackson said smoothly.

Jackson was right. She turned back around when she saw Cyril over everyone's heads. He had a huge shiner! Nishell put her hand over her mouth. That wasn't there at school today! Then Nishell saw Ka'lon. He had a fat split lip!

Nishell was steaming. She got up and stormed over to them.

"Cyril Davis! You watchin' my baby bro. And this is what happens? How you gonna explain this? 'Cause if you don't start talking fast I'm gonna beat your ass," Nishell shouted.

She heard a few titters. Now everyone in the joint was listening and whispering. No one thought she would do anything. Well, when it came to her brother she wasn't gonna let nobody get away with nothing.

"Don't trip, Shell," Ka'lon pleaded. "I cut my lip at school. For real."

Cyril looked around. He grabbed Nishell's arm. He pulled her into a corner.

"Girl, chill. It's nothin'. Let it be. Stop makin' a scene," he said.

"Yeah. That lip ain't nothing. That eye ain't neither. Whatever you been up to, Ka'lon ain't got no place in it. Especially if he starts lookin' like you," Nishell whispered angrily.

"It's cool, girl. Serious," Cyril said. "I was just tryin' to help the fam. The eye was an accident. Ka'lon was out front playin' ball. He didn't see nothin'. And I swear he had that lip before I ever saw him."

"What's goin' on with you, Cyril?" Nishell asked.

"Nothin'. I swear. It won't happen again. You just gotta ease up. Stop nosin' in my business. It's no place for you. You ain't helpin' no one."

"If it's no place for me, then it's sure as hell no place for Ka'lon. We done here," Nishell told him.

She grabbed Ka'lon by the hand and stormed out the door.

She was shaking. Her phone rang a couple of times, but she refused to pick it up. It was probably Cyril.

Ka'lon didn't say a word. He knew better than to mess with his sis when she was this mad. Nishell didn't say anything either.

A block away from home, she checked her phone. It was Jackson calling! She'd forgotten all about him.

Nishell quickly called him back. It went to voice mail. She called again. No response. She texted him a few times saying she was sorry. She felt so bad. Had she ruined everything?

Nishell opened the front door to their house. She pushed Ka'lon inside and slammed the door shut.

"Ka'lon, get your butt in your room," she said in a stern voice. "I don't even want to see your face until Mom comes home. You hear?"

Ka'lon looked at his shoes. He nodded. He knew he was getting off easy. Until their mom came home. Once Ka'lon was safe in his room, Nishell sat on the steps outside. She was still fuming. Jackson still wouldn't answer her calls or messages. She wanted to talk to someone. What was everyone saying about her? Oh, she couldn't think about that right now.

On their way home, Nishell demanded to know what Ka'lon and Cyril were up to. Ka'lon only said Nishell wasn't doing nothing to help Cyril. Ka'lon said he promised to keep Cyril's secrets. Nishell couldn't believe it. Her own brother. Ka'lon would regret not telling Nishell once Sierra came home.

Nishell leaned her elbow on her knees, thinking. What was Cyril up to? She was going to find out one way or another. Nishell had to know where he got all those bruises. Something bad was up, she was sure.

"Hey! Nishell! Girl, whatcha doing?" It was Sherise's voice.

Nishell squinted down the street. It was pretty dark. But she could see Sherise and Kiki walking up the sidewalk toward her.

"Thought you was hangin' with Jackson tonight," Sherise said.

Nishell sighed. She didn't say anything.

Out of the corner of her eye she saw Kiki and Sherise look at each other. Then Kiki came and sat next to Nishell on the steps. Sherise sat on her other side.

"What happened, girl?" Kiki asked.

Nishell figured they'd know everything soon enough. Everyone had seen what went down at Mio's.

"My bro is in trouble," she said. "He was with Cyril and somethin' happened. Neither of them would fess up. I don't know what, but Cyril got smacked up. I couldn't let Ka'lon chill with him! I had to do something. What with Cyril's … problems."

Nishell couldn't stop talking. She almost blurted out that Cyril had been homeless! Nishell hoped the twins didn't pick up on her near slip.

So she just kept blabbing. "I just don't know what to do. I am so *not* into Cyril, either. And now Jackson won't speak to me. It's bad. Maybe I should just skip this whole boy thing. Stay far away from them all. I'll just stick to taking pictures."

Even Kiki knew how obsessed Nishell usually was about guys. "Say what?" she said.

"Nishell," Sherise said slowly, "we heard Jackson was just playin' you, girl. Just showin' you off. First he and Marnyke went on the outs. Then she got a new guy. He heard Cyril was after you. He told Darnell that you must be a dime if you got a football senior after you."

"But ain't nothin' goin' down with me an' Cyril!" Nishell said.

"Even if Cyril ain't after you, you gotta watch your back, girl," Sherise said.

When Nishell didn't answer, Kiki piped up. "Hey, Sherise and I were headed to the club. Friday is teen night. Lord knows we got enough steam to blow off. Come with us!"

Nishell started to say no. Then the thought of Cyril popped into her head. He always did whatever he wanted. It wasn't fair. After she ran out on Jackson, she doubted he was going call her anytime soon. And whatever else she knew about Jackson, he wasn't going home on a Friday night.

Besides, Ka'lon was supposed to stay in his room all night. She didn't want to leave him alone, though. He might try to sneak out with Cyril again. But she needed something to make her feel better about this night.

—

"Yeah!" Nishell said. "I'll come. Gimme a sec, okay?"

She ran to her next-door neighbor's and knocked on the door. Mrs. Henderson was eighty-eight. It took her a while to answer the door.

"Oh, Nishell. What do you need, child?" Mrs. Henderson asked when the door creaked open.

"Could you come over and watch TV at our house?" Nishell pleaded. "I gotta run errands. I'll for sure be back by 11:30. Ka'lon is gonna stay in his room all night. Can you please help me out?"

"No problem, child," Mrs. Henderson said. She grabbed her walker. "TV's the same everywhere."

Nishell helped Mrs. Henderson get comfortable on the couch with the TV remote. Then Nishell ran out the front door where Kiki and Sherise were waiting. Sherise was bitching about how long it was taking Nishell. And they were talking on the phone to people at the club, saying they were waiting for Nishell.

"Sorry it took so long!" Nishell said out of breath. "Let's blow."

The club was only a short bus ride away. When they got off the bus they saw a huge line stretching around the block.

"Oh no! We're never gonna get in!" Nishell said. She'd have to go home before they got halfway to the door.

"Never you mind 'bout that," Sherise said. She hiked her dress up a few inches. Then she pulled a pair of red spike heels from her bag. Kiki and Nishell watched as Sherise grew four inches taller.

"I brought a pair for you too, Kiki." Sherise tossed some black strappy heels at Kiki.

"Like hell," Kiki said. "You wanna wear 'em?" she asked Nishell.

Nishell didn't need to be asked twice. Those heels were smokin'.

She put them on. "Now what? That line didn't disappear."

Kiki rolled her eyes. "It's my sis. Watch and learn."

Sherise was standing next to the bouncer. In her heels she was taller than he was. Sherise put her hand on the bouncer's arm. She laughed. Then she waved Kiki and Nishell over.

"It's her birthday!" Nishell heard Sherise say. "I gotta take her out on her birthday. Can't we please skip the line this one time?"

The bouncer laughed. "You always want to jump the line, Sherise. You know I'm not supposed to let you."

Sherise pouted. "And here I was gonna say when you get off you can come hang with us."

The bouncer shook his head. For a second Nishell thought he was saying no. Then he opened the door to the club. "You always know how to get me, Sherise."

Sherise flashed him a smile and sauntered in. Kiki and Nishell followed her.

Nishell leaned over to Kiki. "Are we really gonna hang with that guy?"

Kiki shook her head. "Nah. He won't be able to find us."

Nishell shook her head. "What do ya mean? Club's not that big."

Kiki sighed. "Just wait till we get inside. You'll see."

When they pushed open the doors, Nishell got it. The bass was bumping so hard Nishell felt in her chest. It was wall-to-wall people too. Nishell could see half the school was there. Everybody seemed to be laughing, joking, and having a slammin' time.

Sherise was surrounded by guys within seconds. Even Kiki's crush, Sean, was there.

Nishell stood by the wall for a few minutes. Would anyone come up and talk to her? She saw Jackson hanging out in another corner.

He saw her looking. She smiled at him and waved him over. He saw, but turned the other way. "Fine," Nishell thought. "I don't need you either." Boys all of a sudden started swarming her.

"Damn, girl, you lookin' fine tonight. Can't take my eyes off those hot shoes," a guy from her English class told her.

"Naw, man," his friend said. "It's that smokin' body she got. You can't take your eyes off her. You ain't tiny like them other girls."

Nishell giggled. "Look all you want. I'm available for the takin'."

"And it's a good thing too. Can I get you a real drink?" another guy asked.

Nishell hesitated. Then shook her head no. Most everybody in the club added something to their drinks. Nishell didn't want booze on her breath when she went home. And besides, she had a big day tomorrow. She needed to be her best. Not hung over.

Jackson glared at every guy Nishell talked to. Nishell decided if he was going to ignore her, she could ignore him too. She made extra sure to flirt with every guy that came her way.

Sherise wobbled by. Looked like she'd had a few too many shots. "Everybody wants to talk to you! You been stealin' my lookers, girl! When you headed home?" she joked.

"Oh, man!" Nishell said. "I'm havin' so much fun. I haven't even checked the time!"

Nishell flipped her phone open. It was almost 11:30! How did time go so fast?

"All right, boys," Nishell told the guys around her. "I gotta split."

A few groans came from the group.

"Hey, now!" Nishell laughed. "You still got Sherise! And don't worry. I'll be seein' y'all around."

She fought her way out through the crowd. Everybody was shouting at each other over the music. She even got stuck behind two guys from school who wouldn't move. She had to listen to their stupid conversation.

"You headed to the fight?" One guy asked. Nishell knew his face but not his name.

"Nah, man. I heard it's a setup," said Lionel from her history class.

Nishell was pushed farther away from them, but she heard the first guy's response.

"Serious? I heard they got some

gangbanger to face Cyril. He'll beat the crap out of Cyril."

Did he just say Cyril? Nishell tried to turn around, but she was being pushed out the door. She didn't have time anyway. She had to get home.

Once she was outside, Nishell practically ran home. The bus couldn't come fast enough. She looked at her phone again. Her mom got off at midnight. That was only fifteen minutes away. Nishell was afraid to even think of what would happen if she wasn't there when her mom got home.

When Nishell walked in the door she found Mrs. Henderson snoring in front of the television.

Her mom hadn't come home yet. Thank God. Nishell felt uneasy, though. It would have been simple for Ka'lon to sneak past Mrs. Henderson if he wanted. Mrs. Henderson was old and couldn't hear that well.

Nishell's phone buzzed. It was a text from her mom. **"Running late. Home 12:45."** Lucky for Nishell. She woke up Mrs. Henderson.

"Oh? What, dear?" Mrs. Henderson asked. "I must have nodded off. So sorry."

"It's okay, Mrs. H. Let me just help you home," Nishell said with a sigh. She'd have to go check on her brother later.

After she'd helped Mrs. Henderson back into her house next door, walker and all, Nishell ran to her brother's room. The door was wide open. He *wasn't* there! Damn! She knew she shouldn't have left him alone. Why would he leave? Did Cyril show up and take him somewhere?

Nishell panicked. Where the hell was he? She opened the door to her room. She looked in her mom's room. He wasn't anywhere.

"Ka'lon? *Ka'lon!*" she yelled.

Nishell was shaking. She pulled out her phone to call the cops. No one liked the police much around here. If they showed up, there could be a blow out.

Especially with her mom. Nishell didn't care. If she had to get help to find Ka'lon, she would. Nishell just started to dial when she saw him.

Ka'lon was at the top of the basement steps. He had been crying.

She came over and gave him a hug.

"What happened, Ka'lon? Where were you?" she asked.

"I ... I ... I was afraid!" Ka'lon wailed. "I went to my room like you told me. But when I came out for water, you weren't there. Only Mrs. H. So I hid in the basement. It's dark down there."

"I know, Ka'lon." Nishell felt so low. She shouldn't have left.

"I needed you, Shell. I was really scared."

"Why were you so scared, Ka'lon?" Nishell asked. "Mrs. H has been over before."

"'Cause," Ka'lon sniffled. "Cyril might come back."

Nishell's face got hard. If Cyril had done something to her brother … "You have to tell me what happened with you and Cyril today," she said. "Right now."

"It was scary, Shell," Ka'lon said. "Cyril said he was tryin' to help his family and the shelter. He said he needed me to do an important job. To come with him. Me! Something nobody else could do."

"What!" Nishell said. Of course Ka'lon wouldn't say no. He thought Cyril was super fly. "What did you do for him?"

Ka'lon shrugged. "Nothin'. It was borin' at first. Cyril went off with some guys. I didn't even notice Cyril's eye. Not until you said somethin'. All I did was play ball. I mean it was okay."

Nishell looked in Ka'lon's eyes. "Nothin' else happened?"

Ka'lon played with his lip. It was bleeding again. "No. Well, they asked me to stand next to 'em while they gave Cyril money. Then Cyril said he was gonna fight some guy. For money. He said he was goin' to give the money to the shelter. It just couldn't close down."

"You serious?" Nishell said. "Someone hit you, didn't they? I'm callin' the cops. Cyril is as thick as bunch a bricks."

Ka'lon pulled on her sleeve to stop her. "No! Honest! I really split my lip at school. We was playin' ball at recess. Cross my heart and hope to die. You can't call the cops, Shell! Pleeeaaaase!"

Nishell stopped. She knew when Ka'lon was hiding something. "There's still somethin' you're not tellin' me."

"I'm scared, Shell. For Cyril. He ... he ... said he wants me to come to the fight. It's tomorrow. Tomorrow night. I'm supposed to hold the money while he fights."

Nishell covered her eyes. A fighting ring? And Cyril wanted her twelve-year-old bro to hold his bets? He probably thought no one would hurt a kid. But did Cyril know what was really going on? A rigged fight! And then what would happen to Ka'lon? He'd be standing there, holding the money! How stupid or how desperate was Cyril?

Nishell grabbed her brother's shoulders. "You don't have to go, Ka'lon. Okay? I promise. I don't want you to even think 'bout it again."

Ka'lon relaxed. "You sure? You'll fix it, right? Cyril is so cool. I don't want him to get hurt."

"I'll fix it," Nishell said. "Whatever I have to do, I'll fix it."

Ka'lon yawned. He rubbed his eyes. "Okay then."

Nishell could see Ka'lon was tired. "Get to bed right now," she told him.

"You don't wanna be up when Mom gets home. We'll both pay then."

Ka'lon nodded. He headed to his room. Nishell sank heavily onto the couch.

"How am I going to fix this?" Nishell thought. And those guys at the club! They must have been talking about Cyril. Did Cyril know he was going up against a gangsta? Nishell had to warn him. She'd figure out some way to do something, without ratting on Ka'lon for telling her everything. Nishell texted Cyril. **"Call me. We need 2 talk."**

Nishell heard her mom come in the back door.

"Hey, baby." Nishell's mom yawned. "What are you still doing up?"

Nishell looked at her mom. She wanted to tell her everything. All about Jackson, Ka'lon, even Cyril. Her mom yawned again.

Not a good idea. Nishell couldn't dump on her right now. Her mom was Nishell's age when she had Nishell. Her mom had gotten kicked out of her house. No help from her own parents or Nishell's dad. Her mom had to make it on her own.

If her mom could do that, Nishell could do this. She would figure this out. She'd let her mom rest.

After today she was exhausted too. Nishell rubbed her eyes and yawned. "Nothing. Just couldn't sleep. I'm gonna try again soon, though."

Her mom started walking to her room. "Good you're home Nishell. Not off to no good like I did. You're a good girl. You help others and have a special talent. Hope you know I'm sure proud. I'm off to bed. I got my other job tomorrow morning."

"Thanks, Mom. Really, it's nothin'. You're pretty cool too. Don't forget I'm going to help at the shelter with the year-book club tomorrow. Good night, Mom."

After her mom went to her room, Nishell put her head in her hands. She didn't feel that good now. It was so easy to lie to her mom. She dragged herself to bed, although it wasn't like she was going to sleep anytime soon. She had way too much buzzing in her head.

If Cyril started a fighting ring, others at school had to know about it. Those guys she heard at the club knew. Word got around. Nishell was sure a whole lot of people knew. How many knew it was rigged? That Cyril was a dead man?

How many of Nishell's girlfriends knew too? Sherise and Marnyke always knew everything before anyone else. Could they have known and not told her? Nishell didn't think so. But after Cyril's behavior today, Nishell knew anything was possible. Maybe no one could be trusted.

Nishell knew one thing she had to do for sure. She had to stop that fight. She stared at the ceiling and began to plan.

Nishell rolled over. "Uhhhh," she groaned. She was so tired. Last time she looked at her phone it was 3:15 a.m. She couldn't stop thinking. And she was waiting for a text back from Cyril. It had taken her forever to fall asleep. She never got a response from Cyril. At least today was Saturday.

Saturday! Nishell bolted upright. She was supposed to be at the shelter today at 11:00! And she had to stop that fight from happening! Nishell had a big day ahead of her.

Nishell looked at her phone. She had a ton of missed messages. But nothing from Cyril. The YC girls were checking to see where to meet before going to the shelter. Nishell checked her phone clock. She was supposed to be there in five minutes!

She threw on clothes. Brushed her teeth. Nishell was barely out the door when she remembered. Ms. O wanted her to write that story for YC. She ran back inside and threw her camera and a notebook in her bag. She rushed out the door again. She didn't want to be any later than she was. Luckily only Tia, Kiki, and Sherise were waiting at the corner.

"Hey, guys. We ready?" Nishell asked.

Sherise rolled her eyes behind her sunglasses. She looked really pale. "Not after last night."

"Sherise had a little too much fun," Kiki whispered.

Marnyke walked up. "We ready to get this show on the road? I want to win at the assembly on Monday. So we'd better figure out what to do."

"Gosh, Marnyke. It's not a competition," Tia said as they started walking.

Marnyke glared at Tia but didn't say anything. "I want to hear all about your girls' night out. My night was a bust. That college geek just wanted to talk about his classes. What a bore!"

Sherise perked up. "Oh, man! Does Nishell have a story for you. She walked out on Jackson!"

"It wasn't like that!" Nishell said.

"Serves him right, whatever you did. That boy has a head the size of Mars," Marnyke said.

"She left him cold at Mio's. After talkin' to Cyril," Sherise said.

"Cyril was just watchin' Ka'lon. That's it. It was no big deal," Nishell said.

"Yeah. Well, he deserved a smack down," Sherise said.

"Ooh, for what?" Marnyke asked.

"For being a grade A dumbass," Kiki jumped in.

"Then what happened?" Tia asked. "I'm really not in the know!"

Nishell sighed. Obviously the twins were telling everyone everything. It wasn't like Nishell could stop them. Tia heard the whole story from everyone's side.

"Well, it isn't your fault Cyril's a thug," Tia continued. "I think we should make something happen with Jackson."

"Like?" Sherise asked.

"Like hookin' him up with Nishell! I don't want him. Hey, I'm on to bigger and better things," Marnyke laughed.

"I don't know, guys ... This fight thing is really freakin' me out. And then we have the assembly Monday. That seems more important than some dumb boy right now," Nishell said.

"Don't worry. It'll be easy. Jackson won't even know what hit him," Marnyke said. She wasn't giving up scheming on Nishell.

"Yeah, yeah. Nishell will have him in her clutches before next week," Kiki giggled.

Nishell just kept quiet. Her thoughts were spinning in her head. Talk to Cyril. Stop the fight. Make sure Ka'lon stayed away. Keep secrets. Tonight was huge. Nishell couldn't think about what or who she wanted afterward.

The shelter was bustling when the girls walked in. Nishell went right up to Francis. "Hey, Francis. We're here! We got a couple more coming later too," Nishell told him.

Francis put his hands on his hips. "Well, I'll be. Never thought you were actually gonna come down. I put you on the roster just in case, though. You girls will all be serving lunch. You're just in time. It starts in ten minutes"

"So we're, like, lunch ladies?" Marnyke asked.

"Sure. But you don't have to. You can sort through the drop-off bags for items to put on the food shelf," Francis suggested.

Marnyke and Sherise decided to sort through the bags. It seemed a little easier. And Sherise didn't think her stomach could handle even looking at food just then.

Nishell said that she'd rather serve lunch. She knew from experience it was way more fun talking to the people in line. Everybody was always joking around. Kiki and Tia joined her.

While Nishell was putting on her apron she saw Darnell and Jackson show up. Sherise immediately grabbed Darnell to work with her and Marnyke.

Kiki watched. "Sherise has got it bad for that boy. He's trouble, though. Heard he'd been through some nasty stuff. At least Marnyke's not hot 'bout it no more."

"Why not?" Nishell said.

"Don't know. She was real mad for a while. But she's okay with Sherise going after him now, though. Marnyke seems to be okay with everything. Wonder what's up?"

Nishell shrugged. "Whatever. Wonder if Jackson will come over here?"

Nishell tried to catch Jackson's eye. He looked away. He started talking to Francis. "Great," Nishell thought. "Francis will have him moving some of the big stuff in the storeroom. Not helping in the food line." Nishell felt like she'd never get to talk to him. And she was a bit nervous about leaving it up to the girls.

Nishell was bummed until they started serving food. She forgot how nice everyone was! Lots of the other volunteers knew the regulars. By the time the line got to Nishell for silverware, she knew a little of everyone's story. She couldn't wait to get out her camera, take pictures, and interview some of the folks.

Finally everyone who came in had been served. The helpers then each got a plate of food and found places at the tables.

"Man. That's hard work!" Kiki said. "And people help like this every week for nothin'?"

Nishell nodded. "A few come in every day. Some people get paid. But for the most part the shelter is broke. They need all the help they can get."

Tia nodded. "Well, it was a lot of fun! So far I've met a ton a people. There was even a guy from my hometown in Mexico. I'd come back and help again."

"We *have* to think of a great fund-raising idea for the shelter!" Nishell said. "Can you imagine all of these people having nothing to eat? That's what'll happen if the shelter doesn't get help."

"Well, then. We gotta think of some way to win on Monday at that assembly," Kiki said.

Nishell agreed. She told the girls she'd be back. She needed to interview some people and get some pictures for her YC story.

Many people were still eating. Many looked at Nishell cautiously as she walked by. She started asking people about their lives. Before she knew it, she had more stories than she could keep track of.

Mr. Kramer was an old man Nishell recognized from when she was young and living at the shelter. He said he only eats at the shelter every couple of weeks.

Every Sunday he plays his saxophone in a band for dance night.

Emily was a woman who had twin baby girls. She was working part-time at a bakery. She said she depends on the shelter to help make ends meet.

Nishell's favorite was Mel. Mel was an artist with a little boy. Most of the time her artwork paid the bills. Sometimes it didn't. When it did, she always came by to volunteer herself.

Nishell felt she had something in common with all of these people. And it wasn't just because she'd been homeless once. They were all just people who were trying to get by. No one seemed like they had given up. All of them still had hope.

As Nishell talked and photographed the people, the other YC members talked to people too. Kiki played with the twins. Jackson loved shooting the breeze with

Mr. Kramer. Everyone looked like they were enjoying their time together.

Nishell was feeling good about the YC visit to the shelter. She took more pictures of the people and the staff. Mr. Kramer joked that he felt like a movie star. He pursed his lips. Then he fluttered his eyelashes. Everyone laughed.

Nishell took her camera to a table way in the back of the cafeteria. She wanted to review the photos before she put her camera away. In case she needed a few last shots. Then Nishell felt a hand on her shoulder. It was Cyril.

"What's everyone doin' here?" Cyril asked angrily. Nishell could see his eye was even more black and blue today. She worried that he was still planning on going through with the fight tonight.

Darnell walked by. "Hey, man. You get roped into volunteering too?"

"Volunteering?" Cyril asked.

"Yeah," Nishell said. "The YC is going to sponsor the shelter for the assembly next week. You should help, Cyril."

"Why you doggin' this? Straight up. I thought I told you to stay out!" Cyril yelled in her face. "You're not helpin' nothin' at all!"

Before Nishell could say anything, Jackson walked up between her and Cyril. "You're gettin' hot, man. Leave a home girl alone. You'd better step off," Jackson said.

Cyril's face twisted. "Fine!" He stormed off without another word.

Nishell was stunned. How was she going to get Cyril to stop the fight now? How was she going to warn him?

"Whew." Jackson breathed a sigh of relief. He sat down next to her. "I dunno what's up, but that guy is bad news. For everybody."

Nishell was so upset she started to cry.

"Hey, home girl. I'm sorry. I didn't mean it," Jackson said, frowning. "I take it back."

"It's not that," Nishell cried. "I found out that Cyril started a fighting ring. His family needs money 'cause they're homeless. He's takin' bets on the fights. He even dragged my brother into it. To hold the cash. Sorry I left last night. I was just so angry. Then at the club I heard that someone is gonna beat Cyril bad. Now I don't know what to do. I gotta stop him, Jackson."

"For real?" Jackson said. "Why didn't you just come clean before?"

"'Cause," Nishell sniffed. "When I was little I used to be homeless too. I was worried if I told anyone, Cyril would tell everyone about me. Then no one would talk to me. You're only talkin' to me 'cause you think Cyril likes me too."

"That's bull," Jackson said. Nishell looked into his eyes. She could tell he was serious. "Promise. I'm feelin' you, Nishell. It ain't got nothin' to do with Cyril or anybody else."

"You sure? You're not playin' games with Marnyke?" Nishell asked.

Jackson shook his head. "No games. I swear. And I'll help you figure this out. We can fix this."

Nishell gave him a small smile. For once she felt like she should just let go. And trust Jackson.

The shelter staff was getting ready to close the cafeteria. It had been a good day. Nishell and the others got ready to go. Nishell was quiet. She couldn't get her mind off Cyril. The fight was only a few hours away. Could she and Jackson stop it?

Darnell, on the other hand, would not shut up. "Today was bomb," he jabbered on. "I feel like I done all my good deeds for the rest of the year! Like, two years even!"

"Darnell, with all the bad things you do? You got like a month," Sherise joked.

She whispered something else in his ear and giggled.

"Guess the two of them are getting along great," Nishell thought.

Marnyke rolled her eyes at the couple. "Oookay then. How 'bout we figure out how to win at this assembly. It ain't like I care. I just don't want to lose to the chess team or cheer squad." She shuddered. "Or even worse. The debate team."

"Hey!" Tia said. "I'm on the debate team."

Marnyke looked at the rest of the group. "See what I mean?" she said.

"Well, how 'bout you guys come over to my house?" Nishell heard herself say. "We can hang. Plan for Monday. Maybe even order a pizza?"

Nishell was surprised at herself. She didn't have time to have the gang over now! Jackson gave her a surprised look.

Nishell shrugged. Now what? Maybe they can get done fast.

They walked back to Nishell's. Along the way, Sherise suggested using the pictures Nishell had taken today at the assembly.

"It would make a killer slide show!" Tia said. "Everybody would know exactly who we'd be raising money for!"

"Great," Nishell said. "But we still have to figure out what we're gonna *do* to raise the money. What are people gonna pay for? We want the whole school behind us."

"What about a carnival?" Tia suggested.

"Nah," Jackson said. "Too much work. And money."

"Oh! I know! A basketball game!" Darnell exclaimed. "People could pay to play with players from the school team."

He puffed out his chest. Sherise looked up at him. That girl had it bad.

Marnyke snorted. "Anybody gonna pay for that?"

"What about ..." Nishell stopped. She wasn't sure how to say it. "Each team or club could do its own thing. So the basketball team could sell one-on-one games. The baking club could sell cookies. Maybe we could sell yearbook space or take people's pictures."

"That's a great idea!" Sherise said. "I'm totally telling Ms. O on Monday. Nishell, you could sell your photographs too."

"People would for sure pay for those!" Jackson said.

Nishell blushed. It made her feel good that her friends liked her art.

"Ka'lon?" Nishell called as they walked in the door. "Some friends are here. Want some pizza?"

Ka'lon came running out of his room. "I want—" He stopped. His eyes got real big. Then he turned around and sprinted back into his room.

"What's his problem?" Sherise asked.

Nishell shrugged. "I dunno. I better go check. You guys order the pizza."

She went into Ka'lon's room. "What up, bro? Looked like you seen a ghost."

Ka'lon was lying on his bed. "I'm not coming out."

"Um, okay?" Nishell said. "Wanna tell me what's up?"

"One of those guys. He's supposed to be at the fight. I saw him talking with Cyril."

"What!" Nishell couldn't believe it! That two-faced, double-crossin' liar! Nishell wondered how many other people out there knew. She was going to find out. "You stay here."

Nishell charged out of the room. "Jackson Beauford!" She got right in his face. Nishell wasn't backing off. Not when he'd lied to her. "Of all the lyin,' two-bit playas. I can't believe you! You *told* me you didn't know nothin' 'bout this fight. You swore. You lied to me. How much more do you know that you ain't tellin' me?"

Before Jackson could react, Marnyke jumped between the two of them.

"Calm yourself, Nishell," Marnyke said. "Somebody is gonna get hurt with that smack talk."

"No way!" Nishell yelled. "He's got it comin.' He's a liar."

"Just chill." Kiki came up next to Nishell. "I think you gotta hear the facts first."

"Fine," Nishell said. She crossed her arms. "He got thirty seconds to explain himself. Tops."

"I don't even know what you're goin' off 'bout, girl!" Jackson said. "I told you I didn't know nothin'!"

"Could somebody gimme the haps?" Sherise asked. "'Cause I am way out confused."

Nishell ran her fingers through her hair. She didn't want any more lies. She wanted Jackson out of her house. Everybody's eyes in the room were fixed on her. Looked like no one was going anywhere till she gave it up.

"Cyril needs money fast. His fam's on the rocks. Got no home. He's gonna have a fight," Nishell said. "Tonight. People been bettin' on it. He's plannin' on takin' the money for his family and the shelter. It ain't gonna go down that easy. Rumors got it Cyril is fightin' a killer. It's rigged. Cyril doesn't know it. He got my little bro in it. Jackson *said* he didn't know anythin' when I told him. Now my bro says a *guy* in this room knew all 'bout it."

One by one all eyes turned to Darnell. *Of course.* Darnell would know! He'd been part of the gang scene in the past. He was a bad boy. Most girls, like Nishell, knew better than to touch him with a ten-foot pole. Even if Marnyke and Sherise didn't. After basketball season ended, he'd gone from bad to worse. No reason to think he wasn't in on all that's going down now.

"For sure," Kiki said. Nishell could tell Kiki was worried for her sister. Sherise always stood up for Darnell. "You know, I ain't seen you do nothin' nice for nobody else until today."

Marnyke went and stood in front of Darnell. "Stop, Kiki. Give him a break. Come on, Darnell. Spill."

Darnell sighed with relief. "Thanks, Mar. I know you always got my back."

"Not right now I don't," Marnyke said. "I'm just not gonna make a fool of myself sayin' things I ain't thought over yet."

Nishell winced. "Sorry, Jackson," she mumbled.

Jackson crossed his arms. He shook his head. "Not me this time. I told you."

Darnell held up his hands. "Okay. So you got me. I know what's happening."

"That ain't gonna be enough tonight," Sherise said. Boy did she look angry. Nishell noticed Sherise's glare was directed more at Marnyke. Guess Sherise thought Marnyke was still playin' Darnell.

"What else do you want?" Darnell asked. "I was just helpin' a homeboy out. I knew he was goin' through a hard time. When he asked to learn some moves, I taught him. When he told me there was gonna be a fight, I gave him my money.

I never knew nothin' about the other fighter."

"For real? Damn." Jackson shook his head.

"So what?" Darnell was angry now too. "Lots a people been plannin' to go. 'Sides, I'm not gonna miss a good show."

"A good show?" Jackson said. "Is that all a homeboy is to you, man? I knew you was in some deep crap, but this? This is over the line."

"Well, what do you want from me?" Darnell asked. "I didn't bet he'd lose."

"Help us stop this fight, then. You want your 'homeboy' getting his face smashed in, or worse?" Jackson said.

Darnell sighed. He rubbed his forehead. "Okay. You right. I'll take you guys there. We gonna put a lid on this mother. We best go real fast."

Nishell thought his last words sounded a lot more commanding.

"Guess the former basketball star gets some credit," she thought.

Nishell watched Darnell put his arm around Marnyke as they got ready to go. Both of them were smiling. Nishell watched Sherise turn away in a huff. Looked like more trouble ahead.

Darnell led the way. "We're only blocks away now," he said. They raced behind some vacant houses. Then through an alley and across some streets.

They had been walking for a half an hour already. It was getting really dark. Nobody said a word. Not even Sherise. She just shot dagger looks at Marnyke. But she kept her mouth shut.

They came up to a fenced abandoned lot. At least twenty guys were walking around in silence inside the fence. Small flashes of light as somebody checked his cell phone or lit a cigarette were the only lights.

"It should be startin' soon," Darnell whispered.

"We gotta go over there! Stop it before it starts," Nishell burst out. She couldn't just sit there waiting. She reached for an opening in the fence.

Darnell grabbed her arm. "We can't just walk in there. Nobody is gonna listen to us," Darnell said.

"I'm gonna go look for the bookie," Jackson said. "Maybe I can convince him the fight is rigged. He'll stop it for sure."

Jackson hadn't gotten more than two steps when the other girls let out a gasp.

Nishell whirled to look. Cyril had come out. The guys were already forming a ring around him. Looked like the other fighter was more than ready to go.

It didn't matter what Darnell said. Nishell wasn't going to let this happen. She couldn't just watch Cyril get beat to a pulp. When Darnell looked away, Nishell squeezed through the fence. She sprinted over to the circle of guys.

Nishell was just in time to watch Cyril get in a few punches. Then the other guy came on hard. He hit faster that Nishell could blink. She saw Cyril crumple to the ground. He didn't get back up. The guy didn't back off either.

Nishell froze. She wanted to scream. The men started pacing around the circle. They were angry. Cyril was down in the middle. Not moving. The fight wasn't supposed to end that fast.

"Hey, that ain't fair!" one of the spectators yelled. He started beating on Cyril too.

Nishell knew if she didn't do something fast these guys might kill Cyril.

All over a few stupid bucks. But she knew she couldn't get those guys off Cyril. Nishell did the only thing she could think to do. She screamed as loud as she could.

All the guys jumped. The men beating on Cyril backed off. They all turned to stare at her. She was very scared but stood her ground.

"You tryin' to call the cops here, girlie?" one guy asked.

Before anything else could happen Jackson and Darnell showed up. They stood on either side of her.

"Okay, guys. You saw what you came to see. Fight's over. Time to leave," Darnell said loudly.

"I ain't got nothing," someone yelled.

"You paid. You got to see the winner. Get gone," Jackson said.

Most of the guys started to move off. A couple stayed.

—

"I want my dough back! Or teach him the meanin' of a real beatin'," someone said. Others nodded in agreement.

It looked to Nishell like this might turn really bad quickly. And now Darnell and Jackson could be in trouble too.

"Look," Nishell said. "If you guys don't leave, I'm calling nine-one-one." She flipped open her phone and held it in the air. She could hit the last "1" in a split second.

A few guys laughed. "Maybe, girlie," someone in the back said. "But they'll be half an hour gettin' here. You may need some help yourself. This ain't your business."

"Yeah. And maybe I know half of you got a rap a mile long. So maybe I hand out some names that'll get 'em here faster. Now I'd beat it if I were you," Darnell told the rest.

Everybody grumbled but scattered within a few minutes.

Nishell knelt down next to Cyril. He was bleeding all over the place. He was clutching his wrist and moaning.

"What happened, Cyril?" Nishell asked.

Cyril winced. "I think I broke my wrist. Don't tell my folks, okay, Nishell?"

"Somebody's gonna have to take him to the hospital. He could have other stuff from the fight," Darnell said.

"I'll do it," Jackson said. "Nishell can help."

Darnell nodded. "Sounds good. I'll get the rest of these girls home."

It took Nishell and Jackson forever to get Cyril to the hospital. They had to hold him up for a few blocks. With his blood all over, it took them forever to hail a cab. When they finally got there, a nurse took Cyril right away.

"You're lucky you got here before the midnight rush," one of the doctors said.

Nishell and Jackson looked at each other. The nurse was right. A lot worse things happened in their neighborhood every day. They were lucky no one got shot.

Nishell and Jackson sat down. They waited to hear what happened to Cyril.

"Man. What a long weekend," Nishell said.

"I know," Jackson laughed. "And it ain't even Sunday yet."

Nishell took a deep breath. It was time. "You know, I'm real sorry about what I said. Back at my house. I just ... I'd be real bent outta shape if you was playin' me for a fool."

"Hey, girl. Forget 'bout it. And right now? I ain't playin' nothin'. I swear," Jackson said.

A nurse walked up to them, "You with Cyril Davis? He's ready to see you now."

They walked into the room. Cyril had a brace on his wrist. There were bandages around his head and chest too.

He smiled when they walked in. "Hey. Doesn't look so bad, does it? Kinda gangsta I think."

"What'd they say?" Jackson asked.

"Broken wrist," Cyril said. "Maybe some bleedin' inside a me. Stitches on my head. Cracked ribs. But it ain't too bad. They're supposed to keep me here all night. I was plannin' on losin' anyway."

"What do you mean? Didn't you know they got some gangbanger to fight?" Nishell asked.

"No. I didn't. I bet against myself and was wonderin' why the odds were so low," Cyril said. "I was gonna give some money to the shelter. Most to my fam. Looks like it still worked out though, right?"

Jackson shook his head. "Naw, man. Had to give most of the cash back. Those guys were pissed. Said you went down too easy."

Cyril shook his head bitterly. "Then this is for nothin'? How am I supposed to get money now? Plus everybody knows I ain't got no home. I don't want no one's pity."

Nishell looked at Cyril. "That's exactly how I feel. I been hidin' from it forever. But that don't make it better. It makes it worse. You're hidin' your real self from everybody. And that don't help nobody. Look at you. You tried to be somebody you're not. Look where it got you. You gotta be you."

Nishell listened to what she was saying. Something clicked in her brain. She gasped. That was it! Nishell knew what she needed to do at the assembly. It would get everyone's attention, she hoped.

"You know, you might have something there ..." Cyril started holding his side.

"I gotta run!" Nishell interrupted him. "Cyril, glad you're okay. Feel better soon! Jackson, see you Monday." Nishell kissed Jackson on the cheek.

She ran out of the hospital at top speed. Sunday was going to be another busy day. She already knew she had to call the shelter and ask them for help. It would be worth it, though. Nishell was going to make sure YC rocked it for sure at the assembly on Monday. Especially with the slide show she could make from the pictures she took. Nishell had a lot to do.

[chapter]

10

Principal Olson spoke into the microphone. "Students! Students! Quiet down, please. Let's have some order, please." Nobody listened. Especially Nishell. She was up next. She was so nervous she could barely breathe.

The gym was packed. Almost every student was there. They'd been there all morning. Most used it as an excuse to cut class. Voting for a fund-raising idea wasn't exactly exciting. Up until the last presentation not many people had paid attention at all.

The last presentation had been the first to cause a stir among the students. It did more than just cause a stir. It brought the house down.

The dance team partnered with the basketball team. Instead of a presentation, they'd done a full-on dance routine. They were bumpin' and grindin' away in front of the entire school!

They were, like, really good. Like a music video. Everybody went wild! Nobody knew what their cause was, or how they planned to raise money. But it rocked.

Nishell was bummed. "Nothin' important really matters at this stupid school," Nishell thought. Then she shook her head. She couldn't think that way. She hoped wanting to help others badly enough would get to at least a couple a folks.

Principal Olson's voice came over the microphone again. "Please. We have just one more presentation for you today. Then you are excused for lunch. Thank you for helping us make our final choice." He looked at his note cards. "And now, the, uh, yearbook club will wrap it up for us. Give them a big hand."

Nishell stood up. Her heart was pounding so fast she was afraid it might jump out of her chest. Out of the corner of her eye she saw the rest of the YC members cheering her on. She'd told them earlier this was something she had to do. Alone.

Standing in front of the mike, she took a shaky breath. It even went through the sound system. Students were still talking. Very few were even looking. But the lights dimmed a little. Nishell started the slide show. Soon everyone was watching. Pointing. Clapping. Whistling. Then the lights came back up. The slide show kept running in the background.

Nishell took a deep breath. She grabbed the mike.

"Hey!" she yelled as loud as she could. The noise made the windows rattle. A couple of students covered their ears. A few glared at her.

She smiled. "I ain't gonna be blastin' any dirty music for ya'll. Gotta figure out some way to get your eyes and ears on me."

A couple people laughed. She could tell everybody else would go back to chatting in a few seconds.

"There ain't nobody in this room who knows what it is to be rich. If we did, we wouldn't be at this school," Nishell started. A couple teachers jumped up. Looked like they weren't happy about what she said about the school At least she got somebody's attention, though.

"We've all got some rough spots in our pasts. I'll call you a liar if you say you ain't. How many of you missed a meal because there wasn't nothin' good to eat?"

A few people looked confused. "Come on," Nishell said. "Let's see your hands." A few hands went up.

"All right then," Nishell said. "How many of you missed a meal because there wasn't nothin' to eat *at all*?"

A lot of hands went down. Fast.

"How many of you ain't had a place to sleep at night?" Nishell asked again. Nobody moved. She waited a beat longer. "Nobody? Okay. Fine. I have." Nishell raised her hand. Nishell took a deep breath. Now for the hard part.

"I was born in an empty crack house. Know why? 'Cause everyone abandoned my mom. She didn't have nobody. My mom grew up on the green side of town, if you know what I mean. Decent house. Big yard. The works. But on that side of town you don't get nothing unless you're perfect.

"Well my mom … she wasn't perfect. And she was kicked out. No family. No community. And before you go judgin', ask yourself what you would do if you didn't have a family. Somebody to rely on. It wasn't easy for her. Before I knew how to walk, I knew which meal was the best one to skip. It's lunch, by the way."

Nishell was hoping for a laugh. But nobody even moved.

"When I was seven my mom found the Tenth Street Shelter, just down the road. Ya'll know where it is. They were the ones who helped us. They didn't give us pity. 'Cause pity ain't good for nothin'. They gave us a bed. Three meals a day. Before that, I'd never even heard of school. Couldn't read. Couldn't write. Hell, I couldn't even add. Without people like them, I would not be here. Pure and simple."

She waited for the jeers to come. The laughs. Nothing. Nishell kept going.

"Now, I know they saved my life. They take care of their own. This community has to take care of their own. I've seen it. Now the shelter is running out of money. Might run out of food. Kids like me? We could be back on the streets in no time. You want to see your baby brother selling crack? You're sister pimping herself for her next meal? 'Cause guess what? That's what happens to communities that don't take care of their own."

She searched the eyes of the gym. Hundreds of eyes stared back at her.

"Now I ain't gonna shake my booty for you. And I ain't gonna offer you cupcakes or ice cream. I don't even want your pity," Nishell said. "All I want is an hour of your time. Or your folks' time. Whatever. But next Saturday, me and the rest of the YC members will be here. Raising money any way we can. Because of the people. The people you don't think you'll *ever* be. They're your sisters. Your brothers. Your cousins. Heck, maybe, even your best friend. They're your family. And don't tell me you're above it. 'Cause you're not. This community needs to stick together. It needs our help. Now. Thanks."

Nishell stepped away from the microphone. It was quiet for a few seconds. Nishell watched as the YC members applauded. Hard. Nobody else did anything. Nishell shrugged it off. She'd said her piece. If the school didn't like it, fine. Nishell turned the slide show to fade. She started to walk back to her seat. She heard the clapping get louder. Then louder. A few whistles came.

By the time she was back in her seat the whole gym was stamping, clapping, yelling. And it was all for her. Nishell knew she killed it. This was the best moment of her whole life.

It was the following Saturday. Nishell's speech had won the idea competition for YC. The fund-raiser was about to begin.

Nishell stepped aside. She watched some girl with a tray full of fresh cupcakes rush across the gym. "Watch out! Hot stuff comin' through!" the girl yelled.

After Nishell's speech, other groups asked if they could set up tables too. The band wanted to have a concert. Even the dance team wanted to have a bake sale. They would give what they made to the shelter. It turned into a big deal at school.

Nishell thought it was cool that everyone wanted to help. She only had one request. Every table was to have a person from the shelter at it. They could help, or sit and just talk. It would help others understand why the shelter was so important for their community.

Now the gym was full of people. And a line out the door was waiting to get in. As the doors opened, Nishell adjusted one of her pictures hanging on the wall. Mel, the artist from the shelter, came over to talk.

"It's so great what you've done, Nishell! Your pictures are fantastic."

"You really think so?" Nishell asked.

Mel nodded. "Better than a lot of photographers I know. You got it, girl."

Nishell smiled. "Thanks, Mel!"

Before long, the YC table was totally surrounded. Ms. O was so proud. Everyone wanted to tell YC how cool the fund-raiser was. Lots of students came up and told her how freakin' kickin' Nishell was to tell her story. Other people came to say her photos were really great. A few people even bought some prints! All for a good cause.

Nishell was explaining to a man how she came up with the idea. She looked around. Cyril was standing at the end of the table. She went to talk with him.

"Hey, Nishell," he said. He'd been missing in action all week. Nishell hadn't seen him since the hospital.

"Hey, Cyril! How you doin'?"

"Still rollin'!" Cyril said. "My dad got a job across town. We got a place to live. I been movin'. Found out I got a scholarship for next year. No big deal. But won't be 'round here no more. How are you, girl? Good I bet. Damn, you got this place hoppin'."

"Yeah." Nishell looked around proudly. "Lot of people showed."

"That's ballin'. I know you'll do good for the shelter. More than I ever could," Cyril said. "I gotta get goin'. I just came over to say thanks. For everythin'. Without you, I might not be here right now. You saved my life, girl. I'll miss you. And Ka'lon. Tell him bye for me."

Nishell looked down. She didn't know what to say. Before she could say anything she felt an arm around her shoulder.

She looked up. It was Jackson! She was relieved to see him. Cyril shook his head. "Be cool, man. Take care of her. She's a dime." Cyril gave Jackson a fist bump. Nishell wondered if she would ever see Cyril again.

"Hey, girl," Jackson said. "You know what I was thinkin'? After this, you and me gotta give that hangin' out 'nother shot."

Nishell smiled. She saw him flirting with one of those dance team girls a minute ago. He must be dreaming if he thought she was going down that easy.

"Maybe. Maybe not," she said with a wink and a big smile. "I'll let you know."

She sauntered off. Behind her back she heard Sherise and Kiki talking. Kiki said, "OMG! Did you just see that? Nishell and Jackson are totally together."

"For real, girl," Sherise said. "We gotta let everyone know!" Their fingers were texting as fast as they could.

No wonder news travels so fast at this school! Nishell shook her head and smiled. She didn't say a word. It was sort of fun to be the center of attention. She would enjoy it for a moment.